D0054239

SAY
"CHEESE"

YEARLING BOOKS are designed especially to entertain and enlighten young people. Patricia Reilly Giff, consultant to this series, received her bachelor's degree from Marymount College and a master's degree in history from St. John's University. She holds a Professional Diploma in Reading and a Doctorate of Humane Letters from Hofstra University. She was a teacher and reading consultant for many years, and is the author of numerous books for young readers.

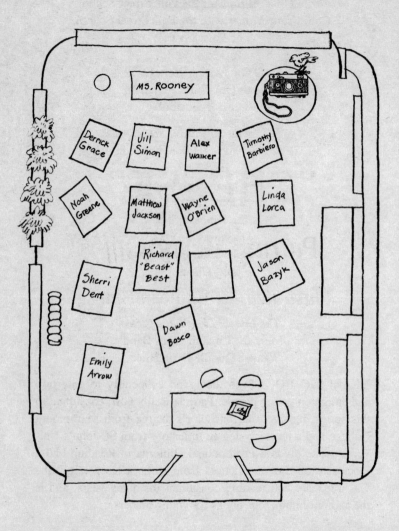

The Kids of the Polk Street School

SAY "CHEESE"

Patricia Reilly Giff

Illustrated by Blanche Sims

A YEARLING BOOK

Published by
Bantam Doubleday Dell Books for Young Readers
a division of
Bantam Doubleday Dell Publishing Group, Inc.
1540 Broadway
New York, New York 10036

ISBN: 0-440-47639-9

Printed in the United States of America

June 1985

30   29   28

OPM

To Ughondi Freeman

Chapter 1

Emily Arrow raced her rubber unicorn across her desk.

"Go, Uni," she said under her breath.

"Line up," said Ms. Rooney. "Two by two."

Emily put Uni in her pocket.

She stuck her hand in her desk and pulled out her looseleaf book.

She held it upside down.

Last night's homework floated out.

So did Monday's math.

But no library card.

"Hurry," said Ms. Rooney. "We have to be there at ten o'clock."

Emily raced into the coatroom.

She opened her lunch bag.

It smelled of cheese.

She dumped the whole thing on the floor.

A sandwich with orange cheese sticking out on the side.

Squished strawberries in a Baggie.

No library card.

"Let's go," said Ms. Rooney. "Last one out close the door."

Emily looked around her desk.

She remembered she was the fish monitor.

She ran back to feed Drake and Harry.

She made a fish face at them.

Then she took a quick look at the skink tank. The skink was sound asleep.

Emily tapped on the tank.

The skink moved his greeny-gray tail. It opened one eye.

Then it went back to sleep again.

Emily hurried out the door.

She was last.

Nobody was left to be her partner.

Richard "Beast" Best and Matthew Jackson were in front of her.

Beast was making shooting sounds. "Pu-quing, pu-quing."

"Good shot," said Matthew. "You got Ms. Rooney right in the knee."

Emily tapped Beast. "Did you see a library card?"

"Pu-quing," Beast said again. At the same time he shook his head.

"How about you, Matthew?" Emily said.

"Nah," said Matthew.

They marched down the hall.

They passed the office.

They went out the door.

"Breathe in deep," said Ms. Rooney. "Smell that June air."

Emily breathed in deep.

But not too deep.

Sometimes Matthew wet the bed.

Sometimes he smelled terrible.

Emily wondered what she should do about the library.

They'd be there any minute.

Everyone was supposed to bring her card.

Days ago Ms. Rooney had told them.

Suddenly Emily remembered.

The librarian had taken her card away.

How could she have forgotten?

She owed forty cents on a book.

She couldn't get the card back. Not until she paid.

The whole library trip was spoiled.

She leaned forward. "Beast?"

Beast was swatting at the bushes. "How come I never find a ball?" he said. "Wayne always finds stuff."

"Lend me forty cents?" she asked.

"Are you kidding?" he said.

"Look in your pockets," Emily said.

Beast didn't answer. He was pushing Matthew into the bushes.

Then Emily remembered Linda Lorca.

Linda owed her two quarters.

She could see Linda at the front of the line.

She and Jill Simon were laughing at something.

Emily quick-stepped up the line.

She slid into place behind Linda.

"Hey," she said.

Linda and Jill turned around.

"Remember those quarters I lent you? For ice cream?"

13

Linda raised one shoulder. "I think I gave them back."

"No," Emily said. "I don't think so."

"Yes," said Linda. "I'm sure of it."

"Listen," Emily said. "I really need—"

Linda shook her head. She turned around again. "I gave them to you," she said. "And that's that."

Emily looked at the back of Linda's neck.

It was long and skinny.

"Noodle neck," Emily told her.

Linda didn't turn around.

Emily walked slower.

She let the rest of the kids get ahead of her.

Now there was a space between her and the class.

Nobody cared that she didn't have any money.

Nobody cared that she was going to be in trouble.

They were all noodle necks.

The line turned the corner.

A woman was sweeping her front path.

She stopped and looked at Ms. Rooney's class.

Emily walked a little faster.

She didn't want the woman to see she was by herself.

The woman looked at her when she passed. She smiled a little.

Emily didn't smile back.

She stretched her head up. She stared at a couple of birds.

Halfway down the block she put her head down again.

She rubbed her neck.

She could see the library up ahead.

Matthew turned around. "I can lend you four cents," he said.

"No, thank you," Emily said.

She sniffed a little.

Four cents was no good.

No good at all.

Chapter 2

The library was dark and cool.

Mrs. Beach was waiting for them.

Emily kept her head down.

She didn't want Mrs. Beach to see her.

She didn't want Mrs. Beach to think about the forty cents.

Emily hurried to the back.

The baby books were there.

That's just about what she could read, she thought.

Little skinny-minny baby books.

She poked her head out.

Mrs. Beach was standing up in front.

The rest of the kids were sitting at the tables.

Mrs. Beach slapped the card catalogue. "The names of the books are all in here," she said.

"In A-B-C order," said Ms. Rooney.

Emily sank down on the floor.

She hated A-B-C order.

Ms. Rooney was always giving them skillions of words for A-B-C order.

"Anything you want to know is right in here," said Mrs. Beach. "Anything in the world."

Emily picked at her red sneaker. The rubber was coming off a little.

She bet you couldn't find out everything in the world.

She bet you couldn't find out how to get forty cents.

She pulled a long strip of rubber.

She let go.

It snapped back against her sneaker.

"Wack-o," she said.

"Young lady," said a voice.

Emily stood up quickly.

It was Ms. Rooney. "What are you doing back there?" she asked.

Emily kept her head down.

She could see feet.

Timothy's sneakers. Wayne O'Brien's work boots.

She walked toward their table.

One seat was left.

She slid into it.

Mrs. Beach started to talk again.

Timothy Barbiero leaned across the table. "Wack-o," he said.

He started to laugh a little.

Emily puffed out her cheeks.

She opened her mouth.

Then she closed it with a pop.

"Fish face," she whispered.

She looked across at Dawn Bosco and Sherri Dent.

They were playing tic-tac-toe.

Linda Lorca and Jill Simon were at the next table.

Linda was trying on Jill Simon's birthday ring.

"All right," said Mrs. Beach. "You can look for books now."

Everyone stood up.

Dawn and Linda went to the storybook section.

Emily watched out of the corner of her eye.

Dawn took a big fat book off the shelf.

It probably had a hundred pages. Maybe two hundred.

Snaggle doodles.

Then Emily saw Mrs. Beach coming toward her.

Emily stepped around the table.

She went over to the card catalogue.

She ducked down behind it.

Suddenly she felt a hand on her head.

"Don't you owe money?" Mrs. Beach asked.

Emily looked up. "I guess so," she said.

Ms. Rooney came over. "How much?"

"Uh . . ." Emily began.

"Forty cents," said Mrs. Beach. She frowned at Emily.

Ms. Rooney reached into her pocket. "Pay me back," she said.

"I will," Emily said.

"Don't do it again."

Emily shook her head. "I won't."

Emily gave the money to Mrs. Beach.

She looked at the card catalogue for a minute.

Then she pulled open the *F* drawer.

F for *friend*.

That's what she needed.

Ms. Rooney was her friend.

But that didn't count.

That didn't count at all.

Chapter 3

Ms. Rooney's class stood outside the nurse's office.

Today was height and weight day.

Emily made sure she was first in line.

She stood up and down on tiptoes.

She stretched her neck as hard as she could.

She hoped she had grown a lot since last year.

After a while she got tired of stretching.

She took Uni out of her pocket.

She raced him along the wall.

25

Mrs. Ames, the nurse, was taking a long time to call them.

Emily tried to peek in the door.

It had frosted bathroom glass.

It was hard to see.

She leaned against the wall.

She thought about her book. *A Best Friend*.

She had read page one and page two last night.

The part about how to pick a good friend.

That's what she'd do first.

Pick someone.

A girl someone.

The boys were out.

Beast was a great boy.

But he was always fooling around with Matthew.

Timothy called people wack-o.

And Alex had picked his nose in reading last week.

Emily looked over her shoulder.

Matthew was tossing a ball from one hand to the other.

He dropped the ball.

Ms. Rooney shook her head.

Matthew dived for the ball.

He crashed into Emily.

"Hey," Emily said.

"Sorry," Matthew said. He scooped up the ball and went to the back.

Emily looked after him.

Matthew looked different today.

She wondered why.

He had on the same old T-shirt.

The same old jeans.

"Ouch," said Sherri Dent. She rubbed at her sneakers. "He stepped on my toe."

Emily looked at Sherri.

Maybe Sherri could be a best friend.

Sherri was a little bossy.

But not too bossy.

Emily remembered what the book said.

Be friendly yourself.

27

Emily put on a friendly smile.

She thought about what to say to Sherri.

The book didn't say anything about that.

"I guess I'm a little taller than you are," she told Sherri.

Sherri didn't look friendly. "I don't think so," she said. "I'm taller."

Emily made her smile more friendly. "That's because you have puffy hair."

Sherri frowned.

"It's very nice hair," Emily said. "It just stands up high."

Sherri stuck out her tongue. It was long and pointy.

"Hair like a giraffe," Emily said. She faced front again.

Just then Mrs. Ames opened the office door.

It smelled of throw-up inside.

"You're first, Emily," said Mrs. Ames.

Emily marched inside.

"Slip out of your sneakers," Mrs. Ames said.

Emily bent over.

Her shoelaces were broken.

She had knotted them together.

Now she tried to pull them apart.

It was one big mess.

"I don't have all day," Mrs. Ames said. "Next."

Sherri Dent came in.

"You've grown a lot this year," Mrs. Ames told Sherri. "I can see that."

"I'm probably the tallest girl in the class," Sherri said.

"I wouldn't be surprised," Mrs. Ames said.

"Puffy hair," Emily said under her breath. She yanked on her lace as hard as she could.

It broke.

She pulled off her sneaker.

She started on the other one.

29

Sherri stepped on the scale.

"Nice gain this year," Mrs. Ames said.

Emily looked up.

Sherri was standing as high as she could.

She was almost on tiptoes.

"Lovely height too," said Mrs. Ames.

"For tiptoes," Emily said in a low voice.

Sherri walked past Emily. "I told you I was taller," she said.

Jill came in next.

Tears were sliding down her fat cheeks.

"What's the matter?" Mrs. Ames said.

"I'm afraid I'm going to get a shot," Jill said.

"Don't be silly," said Mrs. Ames. "Just step on the scale."

Emily pulled off her second sneaker.

She wondered how much Jill weighed.

A lot.

Probably as much as Emily and Sherri put together.

Jill walked out the door.

Emily stood up. She tried to see what the nurse had written on Jill's health card.

Probably a zillion pounds.

The nurse frowned.

Emily made believe she was looking out the window.

At last it was her turn.

"Nice gain, Emily," Mrs. Ames said. "Nice height too. Almost as tall as Sherri Dent."

Emily went outside again.

She knew one thing.

She didn't want to be best friends with Sherri Dent.

And she knew something else.

Noodle neck Linda Lorca was out too.

She still owed her two quarters.

Emily bent over to knot her sneakers again.
Jill wasn't such a hot best friend either.
She was always crying over something.
It would have to be Dawn.
Dawn Bosco.

Chapter 4

Emily stood on the D-O-N-K-E-Y line.

She was reading *A Best Friend* at the same time.

Mrs. Paris, the reading teacher, walked by. "Hi, kids," she said.

She winked at Emily. "Am I glad to see you with a book in your hand!" she said.

Emily smiled back at her.

"You're next, Emily," Dawn Bosco said.

Emily put her book down.

She slid a stick between pages nine and ten.

She rubbed the ball against her jeans.

D-O-N-K-E-Y was her favorite game.

She hardly ever missed.

It was easy.

All you had to do was wham the ball at the wall. Then you'd jump over the ball when it bounced back.

Jill was sitting at the side.

She had missed six times. She had D-O-N-K-E-Y.

She was out.

Emily waited to throw the ball.

She wanted to make sure Dawn Bosco was watching.

"Let's go," said Sherri Dent.

Emily threw the ball against the side of the school.

It came back at her.

She jumped over it.

"Not bad, Emily," Dawn Bosco said.

Emily grinned. She picked up her book.

"My turn," Dawn said. "Hold these?"

Emily took the roses Dawn had in her hand.

June roses.

Wrapped in foil.

"They smell wonderful," Emily said.

"You can have one," said Dawn. "You can give it to Ms. Rooney too."

Emily nodded. Dawn had been a good pick.

She was going to ask her to be best friends at lunchtime today.

Emily went to the end of the line.

She opened the book with one hand.

She read page ten. Then she started page eleven.

Dawn came around in back of her.

"Did you miss?" Emily asked.

Dawn didn't answer. She took the roses. "Ouch," she said. "Lots of thorns."

"Did you miss?" Emily asked again.

"Yes," Dawn said.

"What do you have now?"

Dawn made believe she was thinking. "D-O," she said.

Emily turned the page. "I have D," she said.

"What's the name of your book?" Dawn asked.

"*A Best Friend*," said Emily.

"I read *Ellen Tebbits*," Dawn said. "It has a hundred and sixteen pages."

Snaggle doodles, Emily told herself. Dawn was always saying what a good reader she was.

"How many pages does your book have?" Dawn asked.

"I don't know," Emily said. "I didn't look yet."

"Looks like about . . ." Dawn looked up at the sky. She squinted a little. "About thirty-one pages."

Emily made believe she was reading.

There were only twenty-seven pages.

She had looked the other day.

"I guess I could read that book in two minutes," Dawn said.

Emily turned the page. "I could read it in two minutes too. But I don't like to read fast."

"Really?" Dawn said.

"Really," Emily said.

She tried to read as fast as she could.

Then it was her turn for D-O-N-K-E-Y again.

"Want me to hold your book?" Dawn asked.

"That's all right," Emily said.

"I don't mind," Dawn said. "It's not very big."

"I'm going to hold it under my arm," Emily said.

"Wow," said Jill from the side. "Emily's good."

Emily smiled at Jill.

Jill had a dirty line down her fat cheek.

She must have been crying.

Emily rubbed the ball against her jeans.

Just then the bell rang.

"Go ahead anyway," said Sherri Dent.

Emily threw the ball.

She tried to jump.

The book dropped out from under her arm.

"I'll get it," Dawn said.

Emily dived for it.

She and Dawn bumped heads.

"I've got it," Emily said.

"Right," said Dawn. "You missed, though, didn't you?"

Emily didn't answer. She started for the big brown doors. "Let's go, everyone," she yelled.

Dawn was right behind her. "What do you have now?" she asked.

"D, I guess," said Emily.

"No, you forgot," Dawn said. "You have D-O. Just like me."

"I guess so," Emily said.

She hurried up the stairs.

Some best friend she had picked.

Chapter 5

"June is the best month," said Ms. Rooney after lunch.

She sniffed the roses on her desk.

Emily took out paper.

She folded it into fours.

"It's my birthday month," Jill Simon said.

"Lovely," said Ms. Rooney.

"And the end of school," said Beast. "I hope I don't get left back again."

"Work hard this month," said Ms. Rooney.

Emily picked at her pencil point.

She wished she could sharpen it.

But sharpening time was in the morning.

She tried to think of what she'd write.

"We're going on a picnic," said Ms. Rooney. "In a couple of days."

"Great," said Matthew.

"Great," said Beast.

"I'll take class pictures," said Mrs. Stewart, the student teacher. She used to be Miss Vincent before she was married.

Emily smoothed out her paper.

Dawn:
How about being best friends?

Sined
Emily
(Your best friend)

"Can we bring food?" Matthew wanted to know.

"Of course," said Ms. Rooney. "We'll barbecue. We'll take a bus and spend the day at Grant Park."

Emily looked at the note again.

She picked up her pencil.

We can be bus partners.

"All right," said Ms. Rooney. "Two minutes to get ready for work."

Emily looked up.

She didn't need two minutes.

She was ready for everything.

She folded the note into a little square.

Then she leaned over. She put the note on Dawn Bosco's desk.

"Book-sharing time," said Ms. Rooney.

Emily sighed.

44

She had forgotten about book sharing.

She reached into her desk.

Her book wasn't there.

She took a quick look over at Dawn.

Dawn was opening the note.

Emily hurried into the coatroom.

The book wasn't there either.

She poked her head out of the coatroom.

Beast was raising his hand. "I left my book home," he said.

Matthew raised his hand too. "I forgot to start mine."

Ms. Rooney frowned. "There's still two more weeks of school. Try to get with it."

Emily came out of the coatroom.

She hoped she could find her book.

She didn't want Ms. Rooney to say "Get with it" to her.

Ms. Rooney never said "Get with it" to Dawn Bosco.

"I left my book outside," Emily said. "May
I—"

"Go ahead," Ms. Rooney said.

Emily dashed out of the room.

She hurried down the stairs.

Then she raced around the side of the school.

Her book was lying on the cement.

She sat down and leaned against the brick
wall.

She counted the pages.

Fourteen to go.

That was a lot for two minutes.

That was even a lot for two days.

She'd never do it.

Maybe Ms. Rooney wouldn't call on her.

It would be terrible to say she hadn't read this
skinny-minny book.

And in front of Dawn Bosco!

Maybe Dawn wouldn't want to be best friends.

Emily opened the book to page fourteen.

She read fast.

As fast as she could.

Then she heard clapping sounds.

It was the sixth-grade teacher, Mrs. Kettle.

She was poking her head out the window. "Young lady," she said. "School is inside."

Emily stood up.

She marched around the side of the school.

She kept reading.

She finished page fifteen.

Then she opened the classroom door.

Ms. Rooney looked up. "Good, Emily," she said. "Let's hear from you."

Emily went to the front of the room.

She stood next to Ms. Rooney's desk.

"My book is about best friends," Emily said. "It's about how to get one."

She opened the book. She held it up.

She looked at Dawn Bosco.

Dawn was wearing a new Day-Glo shirt.

Emily wished she weren't wearing her stretchy old T-shirt. It had red and yellow hearts all over it.

"Yes," said Ms. Rooney. "What else?"

"Well," said Emily. She looked at the pictures quickly.

"Emily," said Ms. Rooney. "Did you read the book?"

"Yes," Emily said.

"All of it?"

Emily looked at her sneakers. There was a little hole in the toe.

She could see her green sock underneath.

"Some of it," she said.

Ms. Rooney shook her head. "Get with it," she said.

Emily went to her desk.

She didn't look at Dawn Bosco. Not for the rest of the afternoon.

She was sorry she had sent the note.

Dawn wouldn't want to be best friends now.

And Emily didn't blame her one bit.

Chapter 6

It was going to be a hot day.

Everyone was in the schoolyard early.

Emily looked around.

Everyone but Dawn Bosco.

Emily was one ender on the jump rope.

Linda Lorca was the other.

"Do it even," Sherri Dent said. "I don't want to miss."

Emily nodded.

She and Linda turned the jump rope in a nice wide loop.

51

The rope slapped against the ground.

Sherri Dent jumped in.

TICK. TACK.
CLIMB THE STACK.

Emily took a quick look at the gate.

Still no Dawn Bosco.

Emily was glad.

If only she hadn't sent that note.

Dawn probably thought she was a big dummy.

A wack-o.

Emily's arm was getting tired.

She switched to the other.

JUMP UP.
COME ON BACK.

Sherri tripped.

"Out," yelled Linda Lorca.

Sherri came over. She took Emily's end. "Your turn," she said.

Emily rubbed her hands on her shorts.

She jumped in.

Everyone started to shout:

TEDDY BEAR, TEDDY BEAR.
TURN AROUND.
TEDDY BEAR, TEDDY BEAR.
TOUCH THE GROUND.

Emily stepped on the rope.

"Ouch," she said.

"You're out," said Sherri Dent.

Emily looked at the gate.

No Dawn.

Maybe she was absent.

By tomorrow she'd forget about the note.

Emily pushed her hair off her neck.

The sun was hot.

It was steaming.

She took the end of the rope with one hand.

She patted her pockets with the other.

Everything was still there.

Uni and her lunch money in one pocket.

Two dimes in the other.

The dimes were for Ms. Rooney.

Emily was paying her back a little bit at a time.

Just then Dawn came.

She took the other end of the rope from Linda.

Jill jumped in.

Jill was doing *Strawberry shortcake, cream on top*.

Her four braids were bouncing up and down.

She didn't even get past *shortcake*.

Emily felt the rope jerk a little.

Jill tripped.

"You're out," Linda yelled.

Jill's lips began to wiggle.

"Somebody pulled the rope," Jill said.

"Not me," yelled Dawn Bosco.

"Not me," said Emily.

She didn't look at Dawn.

She knew Dawn had pulled on the rope.

Just then the bell rang.

Everyone had to line up.

Emily ran to be first.

Behind her she could hear Jill crying.

"Wait up," Dawn said.

Emily slowed down a little.

"I read the note," Dawn said.

"What note?" Emily asked.

"Your note," said Dawn. "The one about best friends."

"Oh," said Emily.

She thought quickly.

Maybe she should say she had been working on her handwriting.

Maybe she should say she didn't mean—

"It's yes," Dawn said. "Let's be best friends."

She smiled at Emily.

Emily smiled back.

A best friend.

They went to the line together.

Emily could hear Jill sniffing in back of them.

She swallowed.

She wished Dawn hadn't pulled that rope.

It spoiled being best friends a little bit.

"Let's wait for Jill," Emily told Dawn.

But Dawn started to run. "Hurry," she yelled. "Let's be first in line."

Chapter 7

Ms. Rooney's class stood outside the cafeteria.

The sign on the table said:

BAKE SALE

"Chocolate chip cookies," Emily yelled. "Five cents each."

"Brownies," shouted Dawn Bosco.

"You're going to make me deaf," said Mr. Mancina, the principal.

Then he smiled. He put ten cents on the table. "I'll take one of each."

"Take some carrot cake too," Jill Simon said. "My mother and I made it last night."

"Great," he said.

He put down another nickel.

Emily and Dawn smiled at each other.

Ms. Rooney's class was making a pile of money.

They were going to use it for the picnic tomorrow.

"We're going to have a wonderful time," Dawn said.

"The best," said Beast.

Emily closed her eyes.

She could smell those hamburgers.

She could taste those hot dogs.

Maybe they'd even have enough money to buy marshmallows.

Toasted marshmallows.

Her mouth watered.

Beast reached into his pocket. "I've got to have one of those chocolate chip cookies too," he said.

"Hey," said Dawn Bosco. "You can't do that. This is for the other grades. To make money. Remember?"

"Just one cookie . . ." Emily began.

Dawn shook her head.

"Just one," Beast said.

Dawn turned her back.

She started to talk with Linda Lorca.

"Maybe I'd better not. . . ." Emily said.

"I'm dying for it," Beast said. "I'll give you six cents."

Emily tapped Dawn.

"Beast will even pay six cents," she said.

Dawn raised one shoulder in the air. "He's not supposed to—"

"Don't be a big pain," Beast told Dawn.

"Yeah," said Matthew Jackson. "I'm dying for one of Emily's cookies too."

Emily smiled at Matthew.

She wondered what was different about him.

Dawn shook her head again. "Ms. Rooney said—"

"It's just because we're not buying your brownies," said Beast.

"Yeah," said Matthew. "Burnie brownies."

Emily started to giggle a little.

Then she stopped quickly.

Best friends shouldn't laugh at each other.

Best friends should be kind to each other.

Her book *A Best Friend* said so.

Beast put six cents on the table.

He grabbed a cookie.

He put it all in his mouth at once.

"The greatest," he said.

Some of the cookie sprayed on the table.

"Yuck," said Dawn.

"Double yuck," said Linda Lorca.

Dawn moved over a little.

She stood next to Linda.

"Make some more," Beast begged Emily. "We'll eat them on the bus."

"Yeah," said Matthew. "Yeah."

He put six cents down on the table.

"Give me one too," he said.

Emily handed him a cookie.

In back of her Dawn was making clicking noises with her tongue.

"Wrong," said Linda.

"Double wrong," said Dawn.

Emily took two pennies out of the money box.

She handed one to Beast.

She handed the other to Matthew.

"Cookies are only five cents," she said.

"Beast and I are going to sit together on the picnic bus," Matthew said. "Make a double pile of cookies."

"Want to be my bus partner?" Linda asked Dawn.

Emily turned around a little. She opened her mouth. "Best friends—"

"Sure," Dawn said. "I'll be your bus partner, Linda."

Emily turned around again.

She watched Beast and Matthew.

They were racing up and down the hall.

Any minute the monitor would begin to yell at them.

"Let's bring some candy," Linda said to Dawn. "Half for me and half for you."

"I like Mr. Goodbar," said Dawn.

"Me too," said Linda.

"I hate Mr. Goodbar," Emily said.

But it wasn't the truth.

Mr. Goodbar was her favorite too.

They looked down at the cookies.

The sixth graders were coming along the hall. They'd probably buy the rest.

But Emily didn't even care anymore.

Chapter 8

It was turning out to be a terrible picnic.

The worst.

Even though Emily had a brand-new shorts set.

Pink and green with a pocket for Uni.

Even though they were at the best park in the world. Grant State Park. It had trees and shade and barbecues and swings.

Even though they were having marshmallows. And watermelon.

No. It was turning out to be a wack-o picnic.

On the bus she had had to sit next to Timothy Barbiero. She was the only girl sitting with a boy.

Emily sniffled a little.

She popped a Candy Corn into her mouth.

Timothy had given her four.

Right now Beast and Timothy and Matthew were standing at the barbecue.

Any minute Ms. Rooney would start the hot dogs.

Emily watched Dawn.

Dawn was playing Frisbee with some of the kids.

"Come on, Emily," Sherri shouted. She sailed the Frisbee up in the air.

Jill reached for it.

She missed.

It hit her in the head.

Jill began to cry.

Emily started to walk toward the trees.

She looked back over her shoulder.

Ms. Rooney would probably tell her not to go.

Ms. Rooney was always worried about people getting lost.

"Hey," Linda yelled. "Emily."

Emily didn't answer.

Too bad for Linda.

Linda had taken away her best friend.

Too bad for everyone.

Emily walked through the trees.

It was cool in the shade.

She reached into her pocket.

She took another Candy Corn.

Then she pulled out Uni.

She galloped him across a rock.

She let him rest in the shade.

Then she heard the sound of water.

She walked toward it.

It was probably a river. Or a brook.

After a few minutes she stopped.

She could still hear the sound of water.

It wasn't any closer, though.

She closed her eyes and listened.

Then she started again.

Once she thought she heard Beast calling her.

Then she remembered Uni, still on the rock.

She should have brought him with her.

She hoped he was still sitting in the shade.

She hoped she could find him again.

Suddenly the sound of the water stopped.

Everything in the woods was quiet.

Almost quiet.

Emily could hear the sounds of the leaves.

The sound of a bird.

She couldn't hear the class anymore, though.

It was dark under the trees.

She looked around.

Which way had she come?

She was lost.

Suppose everyone forgot about her.

They'd be having the barbecue.

They'd be drinking soda.

Eating marshmallows.

Mrs. Stewart would take pictures.

The whole class would be there.

Everyone.

Everyone but her.

Dawn would be right in front.

She'd be standing with her new best friend, Linda.

Nobody would see that Emily and Uni were missing.

They might even go home without her.

Chapter 9

Emily was hot.

She was thirsty.

And she was hungry too.

"Hey, somebody," she yelled.

She wished one of the kids would find her.

Anyone.

She thought about all of them.

Beast.

Beast really loved her chocolate chip cookies.

Matthew was a good friend too. He had wanted to lend her four cents for the library.

"Beast," she yelled. "Matthew."

Too bad Timothy wasn't there, she thought.

He'd call her wack-o.

But he'd give her Candy Corn.

A whole bunch, she bet.

And what about Jill?

Jill always said she was the best D-O-N-K-E-Y player.

If only she had stayed to play Frisbee.

Sherri had wanted her to.

So did Linda.

"Linda," she yelled. "Sherri."

She looked around for a stone.

Mrs. Stewart had told them about stones and pioneers.

Pioneers put stones under their tongues when they were thirsty.

She leaned over.

She saw a pink-and-white stone.

It was too big to stick in her mouth.

It would be pretty on Ms. Rooney's desk. Next to the flower vase.

Ms. Rooney would love it.

Emily thought about Dawn.

It had been nice of Dawn to share the roses.

Sometimes Dawn was a good friend.

Maybe not a best friend.

Sometimes she did mean things.

Emily thought for a minute.

Sometimes she did mean things too.

Just then she heard a voice.

"Hey," she yelled again.

It was Beast.

And Matthew.

"Whew," said Beast. "We've been looking for you."

"I found Uni," said Matthew. "I knew you'd be around here somewhere."

Emily stood up. "Hey, guys," she said.

She wanted to tell them they were good friends.

But maybe they'd say she was wack-o.

"You missed great news," Beast said.

"That's right," said Matthew.

Emily picked up the pink-and-white stone. "What?"

"Nobody's being left back," said Beast. "I asked Ms. Rooney."

"I wasn't worried about that," said Emily.

"Pu-quing," said Beast. He shot a make-believe gun up into the air. "I was worried."

They started back to the barbecue.

In front of Emily, Matthew was jumping around.

Suddenly she knew what was different about Matthew.

He didn't smell anymore.

Not one bit.

Matthew must have stopped wetting the bed.

Emily grinned to herself.

She was glad for Matthew.

She was glad for everyone else too.

Now she could smell the hamburgers.

She could see everyone at the barbecue.

Ms. Rooney looked up. "Am I glad you're back," she said. "I was beginning to wonder."

"Ready to take class pictures," Mrs. Stewart called.

Emily gave Ms. Rooney the pink-and-white stone.

Then she lined up with everyone.

Ms. Rooney stood on the end. She held the stone in her hand.

Next to her was Beast.

And then Emily.

"Let me stand next to you," Jill said.

Emily smiled.

She swiveled around.

Timothy was in back of her.

"Wack-o," he said.

"Wack-o," she said back.

"Hold still," said Mrs. Stewart. "We want this

picture to be a great one. Whenever you see it, you'll remember Ms. Rooney's room.''

Suddenly Emily felt a lump in her throat.

The school year was almost over.

Next year they wouldn't be in Ms. Rooney's room anymore.

They'd be different. More grown-up.

''I hope we don't have to go to summer school,'' Beast said.

''We will,'' said Matthew. ''For reading.''

Emily nodded. She'd gone to summer school last year too.

Dawn Bosco leaned over. ''I'm glad you got here for the picture,'' she told Emily.

''Me too,'' Emily said.

Then she thought of something.

After the picture she was going to tell Ms. Rooney.

It was about her book *A Best Friend*.

The book was wrong.

It was better to have a couple of friends.

Different ones.

Bus-partner friends.

Chocolate-chip-cookie friends.

D-O-N-K-E-Y friends.

She held Uni up in the air.

He should be in the picture too.

"Say 'Cheese,' " Mrs. Stewart said.

Emily brushed at the front of her shorts set. She wanted to look perfect.

Then she remembered to smile.

"Cheese," she yelled.